COME ON, G! THE SOONER WE CLEAR UP THE SITUATION, THE SOONER YOU CAN STOP WORKING UP THERE!
ULP!
TO YOU FOR A MOMENT?
YOU?

PROFESSOR VON VOLT IS A FAMOUS SCIENTIST. HE DESIGNED THIS TIME MACHINE FOR THE STILTON FAMILY: THEIR MISSION IS TO DEFEAT THE PIRATE CATS AND SAVE HISTORY!

ZKII ZIIK
SPEEDRAT

...WHILE I WAS LESS LUCKY AND FOUND MYSELF WORKING AT DIZZYING HEIGHTS!
I TOLD YOU NOT TO LOOK DOWN!
MY WHISKERS ARE QUIVERING WITH FEAR!

Geronimo Stilton

WE'LL ALWAYS HAVE PARIS

PAPERCUTZ

Geronimo Stilton

GRAPHIC NOVELS AVAILABLE FROM PAPERCUTZ™

Graphic Novel #1
"The Discovery of America"

Graphic Novel #2
"The Secret of the Sphinx"

Graphic Novel #3
"The Coliseum Con"

Graphic Novel #4
"Following the Trail of Marco Polo"

Graphic Novel #5
"The Great Ice Age"

Graphic Novel #6
"Who Stole The Mona Lisa?"

Graphic Novel #7
"Dinosaurs in Action"

Graphic Novel #8
"Play It Again, Mozart!"

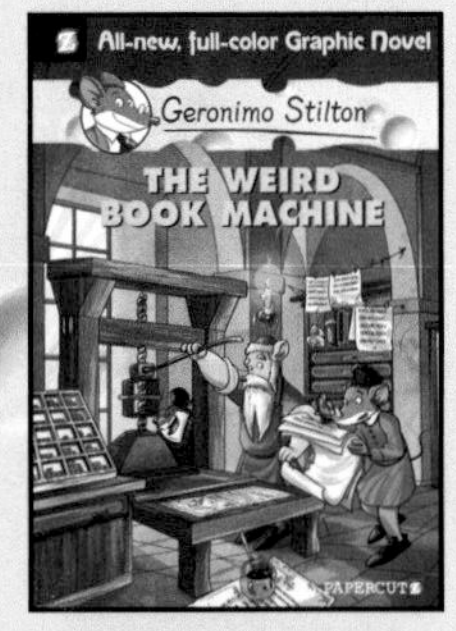

Graphic Novel #9
"The Weird Book Machine"

Graphic Novel #10
"Geronimo Stilton Saves the Olympics"

Graphic Novel #11
"We'll Always Have Paris"

Geronimo Stilton graphic novels are available in hardcover for $9.99 each at booksellers everywhere.

Or order from us: please add $4.00 for postage and handling for the first book, add $1.00 for each additional book.
Please make check payable to NBM Publishing.
Send to: Papercutz 160 Broadway, Suite 700, East Wing,
New York, NY 10038

www.papercutz.com

Geronimo Stilton

WE'LL ALWAYS HAVE PARIS

By Geronimo Stilton

PAPERCUTZ™
New York

Text by Geronimo Stilton
Editorial coordination by Patrizia Puricelli
Script by Leonardo Favia
Artistic coordination by BAO Publishing
Illustrations by Ennio Bufi and color by Mirka Andolfo
Cover by Marta Lorini
Based on an original idea by Elisabetta Dami

Original title: "Il Mistero della Torre Eiffel"

Translation by: Nanette McGuinness

www.geronimostilton.com

Lettering and Production by Ortho
Michael Petranek – Associate Editor
Jim Salicrup
Editor-in-Chief

ISBN: 978-1-59707-347-9

Printed in China
October 2012 by WKT Co. LTD.
3/F Phase 1 Leader Industrial Centre
188 Texaco Road, Tsuen Wan, N.T.
Hong Kong

Distributed by Macmillan
First Papercutz Printing

IT ALL BEGAN DURING A VERY SPECIAL DAY FOR NEW MOUSE CITY...

...SPECIAL FOR EVERYONE EXCEPT ME...
PANT PANT

FASHION WEEK HAD JUST STARTED AND ALL THE STORES WERE PREPARED TO WELCOME INSIDERS FROM AROUND THE WORLD...
YOU WERE A DOLL TO COME WITH ME ON THIS STROLL!

YES, BUT DOESN'T IT SEEM LIKE YOU'VE BOUGHT TOO MUCH?
BUT IT'S NOT ALL FOR ME, G.! I TOOK THE OPPORTUNITY TO BUY A FEW PRESENTS! THE SCARF IS FOR THEA, WHILE THE VEST IS FOR MY SIS-TER! AND THE JUMP-SUIT IS FOR MY NEPHEW!
DON'T YOU WANT TO BUY ANYTHING?

TO BE HONEST, I'M FINE WITH THESE CLOTHES...

BUT CHANGE IS GOOD FOR YOU NOW AND THEN. IT KEEPS THE MIND ALERT!

SPEAKING OF STAYING ALERT, I ALMOST FORGOT! MY NAME IS STILTON, Geronimo Stilton AND I EDIT THE RODENT'S GAZETTE, THE MOST FAMOUSE PAPER ON MOUSE ISLAND!
WAIT FOR ME!

WHY ARE ALL THESE PEOPLE STANDING AT THE CORNER?
MANY CELEBRITIES COME TO MOUSE ISLAND FOR FASHION WEEK. PROBABLY THERE'S SOME DESIGNER WHO'S SIGNING AUTOGRAPHS.

IT'S FUTILE. THERE ARE TOO MANY PEOPLE...

IT'S PROBABLY NOTHING IMPORTANT...

SOMEONE'S COMING OUT!

BENJAMIN!
BUGSY WUGSY!
HI, UNCLE, LOOKS LIKE SOMEONE'S BEEN SHOPPING!

THE PHOTOGRAPHERS HAVE BEEN FOLLOWING YOU?
OF COURSE NOT, UNCLE. WE'RE NOT THAT FAMOUSE!

IT'S JUST THAT PEOPLE SAW WHO WE WERE WALKING AROUND WITH AND THEY ALL STARTED FOLLOWING US!
YES, BUT WHO IS IT?

THERE HE IS! THE MODEL FOR JOHN RATTINI'S NEW COLLECTION!
TRAP?!

CHILL OUT, CHILL OUT! I'M HERE FOR EVERYONE!

BUT TRAP, WHAT'RE YOU DOING?
I'VE GOT A NEW JOB, COUSIN! A JOB THAT'S A GOOD FIT FOR MY TALENTS!

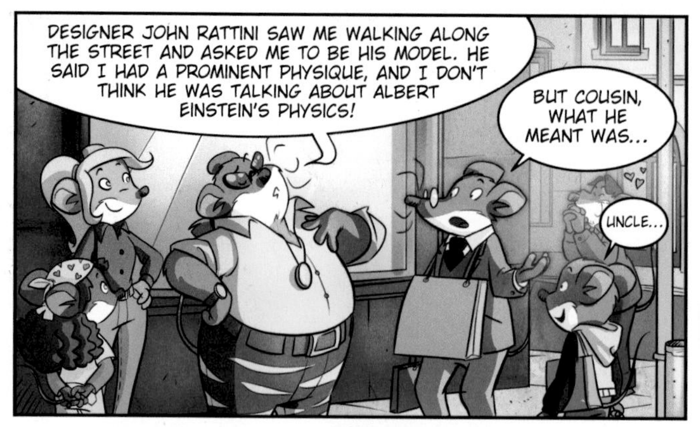
DESIGNER JOHN RATTINI SAW ME WALKING ALONG THE STREET AND ASKED ME TO BE HIS MODEL. HE SAID I HAD A PROMINENT PHYSIQUE, AND I DON'T THINK HE WAS TALKING ABOUT ALBERT EINSTEIN'S PHYSICS!
BUT COUSIN, WHAT HE MEANT WAS...
UNCLE...

SMAK
...DO YOU REALLY THINK UNCLE TRAP IS GOING TO HEAR YOU?

SO RATTINI ASKED ME TO WEAR HIS CREATIONS AND WALK AROUND TO PROMOTE THEM...
GERONIMO! GERONIMO!

ON THE OTHER HAND, GERONIMO, IT SEEMS LIKE A TRAFFIC LIGHT IS ONE OF YOUR FANS!

BUT WHAT A TRAFFIC LIGHT! IT'S ME, PROF. VON VOLT!
PROFESSOR? WHY DON'T YOU EVER CALL ME ON THE PHONE? IT WOULD BE EASIER FOR EVERYONE!

AND RISK BEING HEARD BY ENEMY EARS? NEVER!

NOW DON'T WASTE ANY TIME! THERE'S A TRAIN WAITING FOR YOU AT THE SUBWAY! I NEED YOU! HURRY!

WHAT COULD BE HAPPENING?
I BET IT'S ABOUT THE PIRATE CATS!
DON'T THEY EVER GIVE UP? IF THEY'LL BE GOOD, I'LL GIVE THEM MY AUTOGRAPHED photo!
THAT'S NOT MUCH OF AN INCENTIVE...

TAKE THE TRAIN IN THE DIRECTION OF FIRST CHEESE SQUARE. I'M WAITING FOR YOU!
COMING SOON
HURRY!

NOW WHAT'RE WE GOING TO DO TO GET TO PROF. VON VOLT'S LAB?
IT'S GONE! WE MISSED IT!

THESE ELEGANT SHOES MAY BE GOOD LOOKING, BUT IT REALLY HURTS TO WALK IN THEM!
STRANGE, USUALLY PROF. VON VOLT IS ACCURATE TO THE SECOND!

FORGIVE ME, MY FRIENDS, BUT THIS IS A VERY SPECIAL MEANS OF TRANSPORTATION! AND I DIDN'T WANT ANY MICE OTHER THAN YOU TO GET IN IT!

HERE YOU GO... THE VOLT-TRAIN!
!

TAKE YOUR SEATS! THE TRIP WILL BE SPEEDY, BUT IT HAS TO BE TOTALLY SAFE!

HOW FAST CAN ONE OF THESE CARS GO, PROFESSOR?
YOU'RE ABOUT TO FIND OUT, TRAP!

FULL SPEED!

MOLDY MOZZARELLA!

CLAK

UNCLE, WE'RE GOING TO CRASH INTO THAT WALL!

I DON'T WANT TO LOOK!

EH?

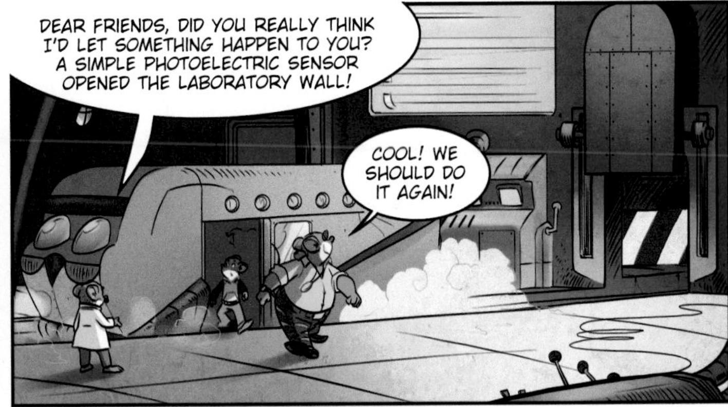
DEAR FRIENDS, DID YOU REALLY THINK I'D LET SOMETHING HAPPEN TO YOU? A SIMPLE PHOTOELECTRIC SENSOR OPENED THE LABORATORY WALL!
COOL! WE SHOULD DO IT AGAIN!

GERONIMO, TIME IS PRESSING. THE CATS HAVE GONE INTO ACTION! THEY'RE SURE TO WANT TO CHANGE THE PAST TO THEIR ADVANTAGE.
WHERE ARE THEY RIGHT NOW?
OH...

THE TEMPOGRAPH SHOWS THAT THEY WENT TO PARIS IN 1889, EVEN THOUGH WHY THEY'VE GONE THERE IS STILL A MYSTERY.

COULD IT BE FOR THE CONSTRUCTION OF THE EIFFEL TOWER? IT WAS UNVEILED THAT VERY YEAR.

THAT'S WHAT I THOUGHT, BUT I'M NOT SURE ABOUT IT. ONCE YOU ARRIVE IN PARIS, I SUGGEST YOU CONTACT THE BUILDER OF THE TOWER, GUSTAVE EIFFEL, AND SEE IF SOMETHING'S WRONG!
MY GOOD OLD SPEEDRAT! I'LL DRIVE!

YOU'LL FIND EVERYTHING YOU NEED FOR THE MISSION INSIDE THE SPEEDRAT. BE CAREFUL, THE PIRATE CATS ARE DANGEROUS!

MEANWHILE, THE PIRATE CATS HAD ARRIVED IN PARIS IN 1889...

*CALM DOWN!

BONZO! WHAT ARE YOU DOING?!
UMM... NOTHING...

I TOLD YOU TO DO THIS BEFORE WE LEFT! I CAN'T BELIEVE YOU ALWAYS LEAVE THINGS TO THE LAST SECOND!
BUT I SPENT THE LAST WEEK SEWING THE CLOTHES FOR THE MISSION...

EVERY COMMAND GIVEN BY THE EMPEROR OF THE PIRATE CATS MUST BE CARRIED OUT IMMEDIATELY!
BUT IF I HADN'T LET OUT YOUR CLOTHING, YOU NEVER WOULD'VE BEEN ABLE TO PUT ON THOSE PANTS!
HOW DARE YOU TREAT ME WITH SUCH DISRESPECT!
MEOW DOWN*!
*CALM DOWN!

IN THE MEANTIME, WE'LL LEAVE THIS HERE. IF WE BRING A BOOK FROM THE FUTURE WITH US WE'LL BE DISCOVERED!

LET'S GO. GUSTAVE EIFFEL AND PARIS AWAIT US!

MEANWHILE, WE, TOO, HAD ARRIVED AT OUR DESTINATION-- BUT WE WERE HAVING LOTS OF PROBLEMS...
UNCLE GERONIMO, HOW ARE WE GOING TO GET CLOSE TO GUSTAVE EIFFEL?
WE'RE ALMOST AT THE FIELD OF MARS. THE TOWER CONSTRUCTION SITE IS JUST BEYOND IT. WE'LL TRY TO FIND HIM THERE.
MARS? BUT THEN WE SHOULD'VE TAKEN A SPACESHIP, NOT THE SPEEDRAT!

NO, TRAP. THE FIELD OF MARS IS JUST A PARK IN PARIS.
THE FIELD OF MARS GETS ITS NAME FROM THE MARS FIELD, AN ANCIENT PART OF ROME DEDICATED TO THE GOD OF WAR, MARS. THE FIELD OF MARS WAS CONSTRUCTED BY LOUIS XV IN THE 18TH CENTURY AS A SITE FOR THE MILITARY SCHOOL TO PRACTICE MANEUVERS. TODAY IT HAS BECOME A PUBLIC GARDEN SUBDIVIDED BY FLOWER BEDS, WITH ARCHES, WATERFALLS, A POOL, AND WIDE PATHS INSIDE IT.

I'M SURE MR. EIFFEL WILL BE AT THE SITE. WE JUST HAVE TO...
HALT!

STATE YOUR BUSINESS HERE.
UHM, ACTUALLY, WE HAVE TO...
WE'RE HERE TO MEET MONSIEUR. EIFFEL. CAN YOU SHOW US WHERE HIS TENT IS?

DO YOU HAVE AN APPOINTMENT? ARE YOU WORKING AT THE CONSTRUCTION SITE? MONSIEUR EIFFEL IS VERY BUSY AND CAN'T SPEAK TO ALL THE WORKERS EMPLOYED IN THE CONSTRUCTION.

OH! BUT WE'RE NOT WORKERS! WE REALLY HAVE NOTHING TO DO WITH BUILDING THE TOWER!

--IF YOU'RE NOT INVOLVED IN THE CONSTRUCTION, YOU CAN'T ENTER THE CONSTRUCTION SITE, LET ALONE TALK TO MONSIEUR EIFFEL!
THANKS A LOT, COUSIN!
OH...

OUR MISSION IS TURNING OUT TO BE MORE COMPLICATED THAT I'D THOUGHT...
AND WE CAN'T EVEN SNEAK INTO THE CONSTRUCTION SITE, NOW THAT THE GUARD KNOWS WE DON'T WORK HERE!
NOW WHAT'LL WE DO?

HELP WANTED
I MIGHT HAVE AN IDEA...

THE FIRST ***WORLD EXPOSITION*** TOOK PLACE IN LONDON IN 1851. TODAY, WORLD'S FAIRS TAKE PLACE IN DIFFERENT COUNTRIES EVERY FIVE YEARS. THE 1889 WORLD'S FAIR OCCURRED IN PARIS FROM MAY 6 TO OCTOBER 31, TO CELEBRATE THE CENTENARY OF THE FRENCH REVOLUTION. IT INVOLVED 32 NATIONS OF THE WORLD AND ATTRACTED 32 MILLION SPECTATORS.

GUSTAVE EIFFEL (1832-1923), FRENCH ENGINEER AND BUSINESSMAN, IS PRIMARILY KNOWN FOR HAVING CREATED THE TOWER THAT BEARS HIS NAME, BUT DURING HIS CAREER HE DESIGNED OVER 150 PROJECTS MADE OF IRON ALL OVER THE WORLD, INCLUDING THE INTERNAL STRUCTURE OF THE CELEBRATED STATUE OF LIBERTY IN NEW YORK.

BUT WHY ENTER FROM OVER THERE?
OH, NO REASON. THERE WAS A GUARD WHO DIDN'T WANT TO LET ME IN.
AND SO THAT'S WHY...

BUT LET'S NOT TALK ABOUT ME! LET'S TALK ABOUT MY PROJECTS!
PROJECTS?

I ACCIDENTALLY HEARD YOUR DISCUSSION WITH THE EXPO ORGANIZERS. QUITE A PROBLEM, THAT ASPARAGUS, EH?
RIGHT... THEY CAN COMPLAIN ALL THEY WANT BUT IT'S TOO LATE TO CHANGE THE TOWER! DESIGNING A NEW ONE WOULD TAKE TOO MUCH TIME...

BUT IF SOMEONE WERE TO HAVE... I DON'T KNOW, AN IDEA, ABOUT HOW TO MODIFY THE PROJECT...
YOU?

LISTEN, MONSIEUR DE BUILDING, I HAVE NEITHER THE TIME NOR THE DESIRE TO STAY AND HEAR YOUR IDEAS...
WAIT!

JUST TAKE A LOOK HERE. YOU'LL SEE SOMETHING THAT'LL AMAZE YOU!

BUT... BUT...

BUT YOU...

BUT YOU'RE A GENIUS!

OF COURSE, THE WAY YOU'VE DESIGNED IT IS TERRIFIC, BUT THE IDEAS IT'S BASED ON ARE VISIONARY!

I DON'T KNOW, HOWEVER, HOW YOUR IDEAS CAN BE APPLIED TO MY TOWER. WE STILL NEED THE RIGHT PROJECT...

I JUST HAD ONE THAT MIGHT BE EXACTLY WHAT WE NEED... BUT WHERE IS IT?

HERE IT IS: "THE GHERKIN."

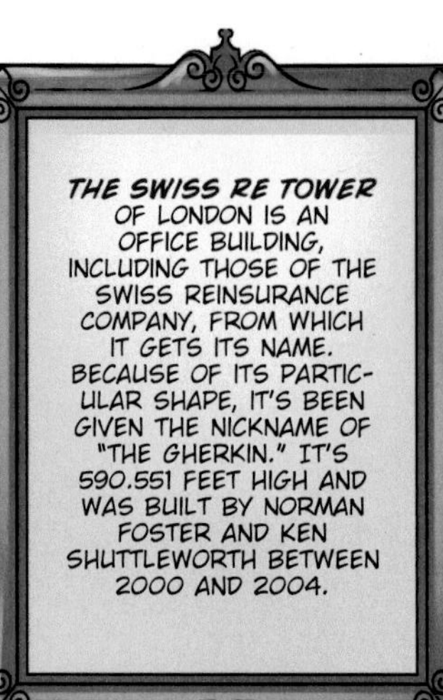
THE SWISS RE TOWER OF LONDON IS AN OFFICE BUILDING, INCLUDING THOSE OF THE SWISS REINSURANCE COMPANY, FROM WHICH IT GETS ITS NAME. BECAUSE OF ITS PARTICULAR SHAPE, IT'S BEEN GIVEN THE NICKNAME OF "THE GHERKIN." IT'S 590.551 FEET HIGH AND WAS BUILT BY NORMAN FOSTER AND KEN SHUTTLEWORTH BETWEEN 2000 AND 2004.

IT'S A BOLD PROJECT, BUT I DON'T SEE HOW IT COULD BE USEFUL TO OUR CURRENT SITUATION. WE CAN'T KNOCK DOWN SOMETHING WE'VE ALREADY BUILT!

NATURALLY! BUT I KNOW YOU ALSO BUILT THE INTERNAL FRAME OF THE AMERICAN STATUE OF LIBERTY. OUR PROJECT WOULD BE SIMILAR.
IT WOULD BE ENOUGH TO USE "YOUR" TOWER AS THE SHELL FOR "MY" TOWER! THAT WAY YOUR WORK WOULDN'T BE WASTED!
LIKE THIS?
EXACTLY!

OF COURSE, MAKING SOME MODIFICATIONS HERE AND THERE...
I THINK IT WOULD BE AN UNPARALLELED SIGHT!

MEANWHILE WE'D MANAGED TO GET INTO THE WORK SITE...
PATTY WAS IN CHARGE OF BUILDING SUPPLIES...
TOMORROW THE NEW BOLTS SHOULD ARRIVE TO REPLACE THOSE DEFECTIVE ONES.
GOOD, THEY WERE LATE!

...WHILE I WAS LESS LUCKY AND FOUND MYSELF WORKING AT DIZZYING HEIGHTS!
I TOLD YOU NOT TO LOOK DOWN!
MY WHISKERS ARE QUIVERING WITH FEAR!

OBVIOUSLY, TRAP WAS THE ONLY ONE HAVING A GOOD TIME!
COMING THROUGH!

WATCH OUT! I'VE GOT PIECES OF GLOWING HOT IRON!

THESE WHEELBARROW RUNS ARE REALLY FUN!

HEY, G... HOW'S IT GOING?
WHEN THEY ASKED ME IF I SUFFERED FROM VERTIGO, I THOUGHT THEY WERE TALKING ABOUT CLIMBING UP A LADDER, NOT WORKING AT A HEIGHT OF 820 FEET!
WERE YOU ABLE TO FIND EIFFEL?

I ASKED AROUND. THAT'S HIS TENT! LOOK, HE'S COMING OUT!

COME ON, G! THE SOONER WE CLEAR UP THE SITUATION, THE SOONER YOU CAN STOP WORKING UP THERE!
ULP!

UHM... MONSIEUR EIFFEL, COULD I SPEAK TO YOU FOR A MOMENT?
AND WHO ARE YOU?

MY NAME IS JERRY DE RATTY. I WORK ON THE WEST SIDE OF THE TOWER...

DON'T WASTE THE MASTER'S TIME! IF YOU WANT SOMETHING, ASK THE CARPENTRY SUPERVISOR!
BUT I COULD FIND A MOMENT...
BUT... BUT...
DON'T EVEN THINK ABOUT IT!

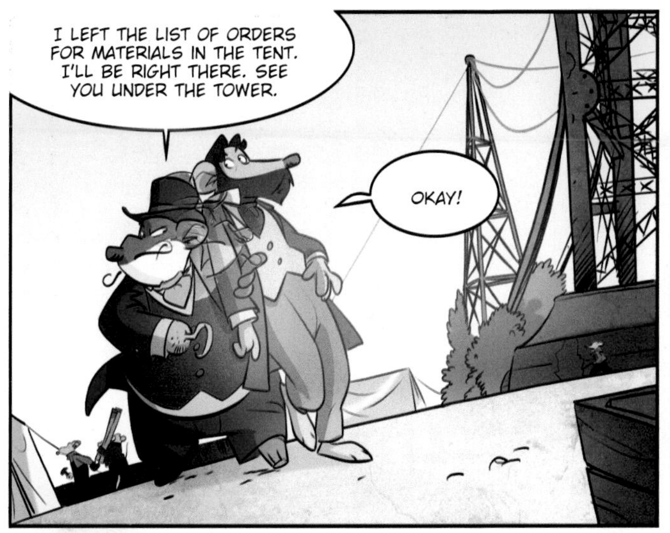

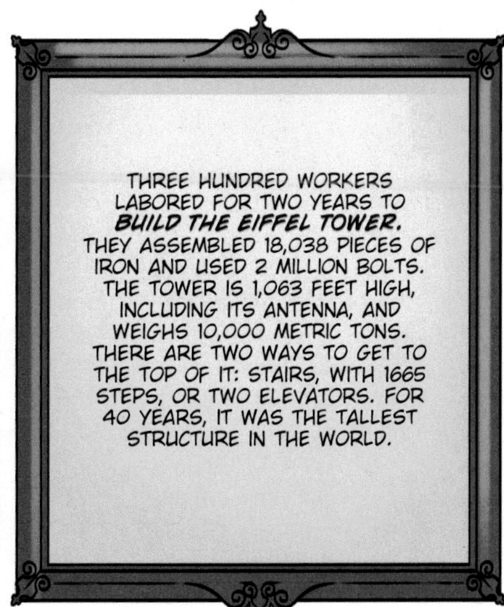

THREE HUNDRED WORKERS LABORED FOR TWO YEARS TO ***BUILD THE EIFFEL TOWER.*** THEY ASSEMBLED 18,038 PIECES OF IRON AND USED 2 MILLION BOLTS. THE TOWER IS 1,063 FEET HIGH, INCLUDING ITS ANTENNA, AND WEIGHS 10,000 METRIC TONS. THERE ARE TWO WAYS TO GET TO THE TOP OF IT: STAIRS, WITH 1665 STEPS, OR TWO ELEVATORS. FOR 40 YEARS, IT WAS THE TALLEST STRUCTURE IN THE WORLD.

WHEN I SAY SO, DROP THOSE GIRDERS AND WE'LL GET RID OF THOSE SUFFERING SQUEAKERS!
NHNN

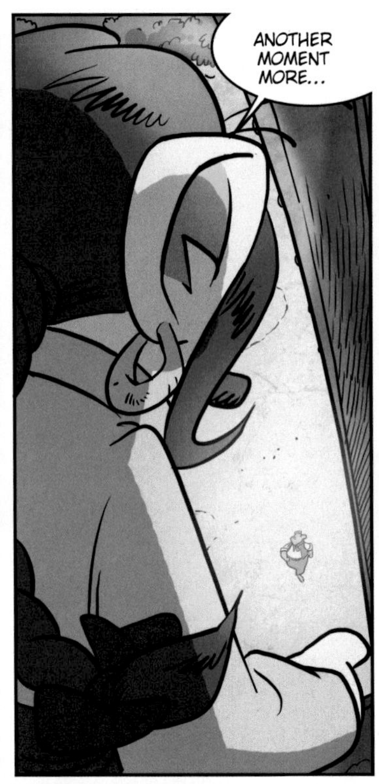
ANOTHER MOMENT MORE...

NOW!
BUT WHERE ARE THEY?

BLAMM
?!

THERE THEY ARE! JUST WHAT I WAS LOOKING FOR!

YOU STUPID CAT!
BUT I JUST FOLLOWED YOUR ORDERS!

OTHER ATTEMPTS DIDN'T TURN OUT WELL EITHER...
HE WAS RIGHT ON THE TRACK. HOW DID YOU MANAGE TO MISS HIM?
OWIE, OWIE, OWIE...

THE CATWALK WAS SUPPOSED TO SNAP FROM HIS WEIGHT, NOT YOURS!
CAN WE TALK ABOUT THIS WHEN I'M NOT ABOUT TO BECOME MASHED MOUSE?

ENOUGH, I GIVE UP! EVEN THE SIMPLEST PLANS BECOME IMPOSSIBLE WITH YOU!
I DON'T FEEL VERY GOOD...

WE'D DO BETTER TO PUT OUR EFFORTS INTO SOMETHING MORE PRODUCTIVE. SOON THE RATS WON'T BE ABLE TO KEEP OUR PLAN FROM SUCCEEDING.
I REALLY DON'T FEEL VERY GOOD...

WITH TIME SO TIGHT, ALL THE WORKERS WERE FORCED TO TAKE ON BACK-BREAKING SHIFTS...
UNCLE, ARE YOU GOING TO GET UP?
SOME WERE USED TO IT OTHERS, LESS SO...

BETWEEN THE DIZZINESS AND THE FATIGUE, I THINK I'LL STAY HERE ANOTHER FIVE MINUTES...

COUSIN, QUICK! WE'LL BE LATE FOR DINNER!
HOW COME YOU'RE NOT TIRED? WE'RE WORKING ENDLESS SHIFTS!
WELL, IN THE WAREHOUSE, YOU JUST HAVE TO KEEP THE ACCOUNTS IN ORDER. IT'S NO BIG DEAL!
AND YOU, TRAP? YOU'RE IN PERFECT SHAPE. HOW DO YOU DO IT?
TO TELL THE TRUTH...

"FIRST I CARRIED BOLTS, BUT THEY TOLD ME I WAS WASTED AT THAT...

"...THEN THEY HAD ME COORDINATE THE WORK ON THE EAST SIDE...

"...FINALLY, THEY DECIDED I WAS BEST SUITED FOR THE TASK OF SUPERVISING!"

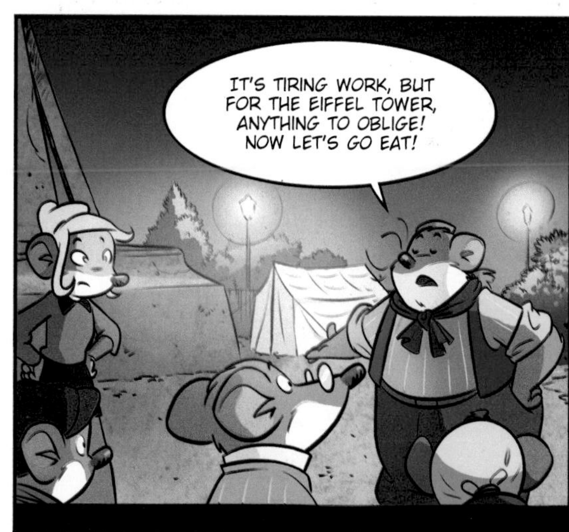
IT'S TIRING WORK, BUT FOR THE EIFFEL TOWER, ANYTHING TO OBLIGE! NOW LET'S GO EAT!

HEY! WHERE'S MY HAMMER?

YOU LEFT IT IN THE TOWER. WHEN YOU GOT HERE, YOU DIDN'T HAVE IT WITH YOU!

OH, NO! I HAVE TO GO BACK TO THE TOWER!
AND IN A HURRY, TOO! IF YOU DON'T BRING IT BACK TO THE WAREHOUSE, YOU'LL BE IN BIG TROUBLE! THEY'RE VERY STRICT ABOUT WORK TOOLS!

WE'LL GO GET IT! I KNOW WHERE YOU WERE WORKING. IT WON'T TAKE LONG TO FIND IT. AND YOU CAN REST A BIT LONGER!
HMM...

WE'LL BE CAREFUL, I PROMISE!
THE AREA IS WELL-LIT. PLUS YOU WERE WORKING IN A SAFE AREA TODAY!
OKAY...

IT'LL JUST TAKE US A MOMENT. WE'LL BE RIGHT BACK.
BE CAREFUL!

WE'RE FINALLY GOING TO GET TO GO IN THE TOWER! UNTIL NOW WE'VE JUST SEEN THE WAREHOUSE!
LET'S GRAB THE HAMMER AND GO RIGHT BACK: WE CAN'T DELAY TRAP'S DINNER! HEE HEE HEE!

HUH?

THERE'S SOMEONE THERE...

THAT'S STRANGE. THEY SHOULD ALL BE AT DINNER NOW...

MAYBE ONE OF THEM ALSO FORGOT SOMETHING...
THAT MAY BE, BUT ALL THAT MOVEMENT IS SUSPICIOUS. WE'D BETTER CHECK!

HURRY OR WE'LL LOSE THEM!

THEY'RE GOING UP.

I KNOW UNCLE TOLD US TO BE QUICK, BUT IF IT'S THE PIRATE CATS, WE HAVE TO DISCOVER THEIR PLAN!
IT'S TOO IMPORTANT! LET'S FOLLOW THEM!

LUCKILY THE LOWER PART OF THE TOWER IS FINISHED NOW, SO IT'S SAFE!
COME ON, WE'RE ALMOST THERE!

HERE'S THE LIGHT WE WERE FOLLOWING!
BUT NO ONE'S HERE!

THE SOUND OF FOOTSTEPS! THEY'RE COMING BACK! QUICK, LET'S HIDE!

WE'D BETTER BE ABSOLUTELY SILENT!

THE WORK IS MOVING ALONG. IT'S EASIER THAN WE THOUGHT!
RIGHT, AND THOSE INSUFFERABLE STILTON SQUEAKERS DON'T HAVE ANY IDEA WHAT OUR PLAN IS!
WHY HAVEN'T YOU ELIMINATED THEM ALREADY?
ERRMM... TO TELL THE TRUTH...

...WE DIDN'T SUCC... OW!
WE THOUGHT ABOUT IT FOR A LONG TIME AND DECIDED IT WASN'T WORTH IT.

WHAT DO YOU MEAN?
IF WE KNOCKED THE STILTONS OUT OF THE GAME, WORK WOULD CEASE, AND WE'D PUT EVERYONE ON THE ALERT.

YOU'RE RIGHT. THEY CAN STICK THEIR NOSES INTO WHATEVER THEY WISH, BUT THEY'LL NEVER FIGURE OUT WHAT WE WANT TO DO!

RIGHT! OUR PLAN IS SO SECRET THEY'LL NEVER GET IT...

WELL, IT'S SO SECRET THAT I DON'T EVEN UNDERSTAND IT MYSELF...

WHY DID YOU HAVE ME COPY THOSE FAMOUS 20TH CENTURY BUILDINGS IN SUCH A RUSH?
I NEEDED TO CONVINCE EIFFEL THAT I WAS A BRILLIANT ARCHITECT AND THAT I COULD HELP HIM FIX HIS WORK...

AND THAT WAY I WAS ABLE TO PUT MY EVEN MORE BRILLIANT PLAN INTO ACTION!

I PUT NEW SECTIONS IN, WITH EXPLOSIVES. THAT WILL ALLOW US TO TRANSFORM THE EIFFEL TOWER INTO THE GREATEST MONUMENT EVER RECORDED IN HISTORY!

THE GARGANTUAN TOWER OF CATARDONE III OF CATATONIA, THE GREAT EMPEROR OF THE CATS!

?!

UMM... GARGANTUAN?

THAT MEANS "GIGANTIC," "ENORMOUS."
OH, WELL, THEN IT WILL BE PRETTY FAITHFUL TO THE ORIGINAL, HA, HA, HA!

I'M GOING TO ATOMIZE YOU!*
LET'S GO NOW!
*DESTROY YOU!

LET'S HIGHTAIL IT! WE HAVE TO WARN UNCLE GERONIMO RIGHT AWAY!

UNCLE! UNCLE! THE CATS!
WHERE HAVE YOU BEEN? WE'VE BEEN WORRIED!

WHAT HAPPENED?

WE DISCOVERED THAT CATARDONE IS WORKING ON THE CONSTRUCTION OF THE TOWER. AND HE WANTS TO CREATE A STATUE IN HIS IMAGE AND LIKENESS!
AND HOW IS CATARDONE GOING TO LOOK LIKE A TOWER?

HE SAID HE'D PUT EXPLOSIVES IN THE TOWER, TO BLOW UP THE PIECES NEEDED TO TRANSFORM THE TOWER!

THE SITUATION IS MORE SERIOUS THAN WE EXPECTED. THIS TIME I DON'T THINK WE CAN DO THIS ALONE...
WHAT DO YOU MEAN, G?

WE NEED PROF. VON VOLT!

TRAP, YOU STAY HERE WITH BENJAMIN AND BUGSY WUGSY! PETUNIA AND I'LL RETURN TO THE SPEEDRAT AND GO TALK TO VON VOLT. THERE'S NOT A MOMENT TO LOSE!
AGREED!
AGREED!

A LITTLE LATER...
WE'VE NEVER GOTTEN TO THIS POINT BEFORE! THERE'S A GOOD CHANCE THE PIRATE CATS WILL WIN!
CALM DOWN, G.! VON VOLT WILL HAVE A SOLUTION!

TAKEOFF!

TWO HUNDRED YEARS LATER IN THE FUTURE...
NICE LANDING, G.!
I'M BEGINNING TO APPRECIATE TRAP AS A PILOT...
GERONIMO?! HOW'D IT GO? AND THE OTHERS?

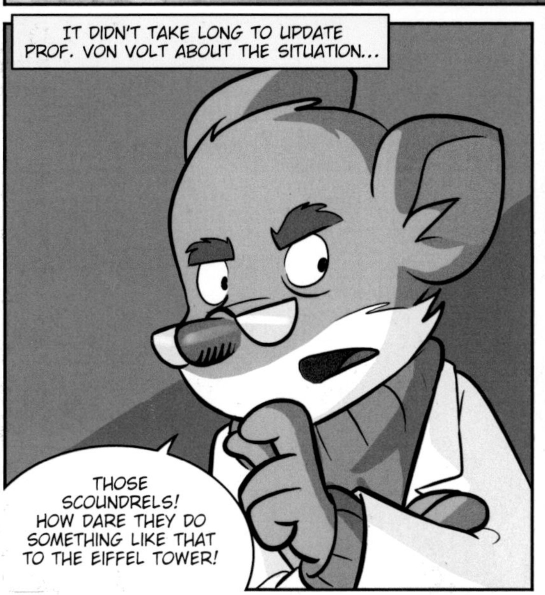
IT DIDN'T TAKE LONG TO UPDATE PROF. VON VOLT ABOUT THE SITUATION...
THOSE SCOUNDRELS! HOW DARE THEY DO SOMETHING LIKE THAT TO THE EIFFEL TOWER!

WE NEED YOUR ADVICE TO AVERT THIS THREAT.

THEIR PLANS ARE BECOMING MORE COMPLEX, AND AS A RESULT, MORE DIFFICULT TO BLOCK...

...IF WE REVEAL THE TRUTH, WE'LL ALSO HAVE TO SAY THAT THEIR AND OUR KNOWLEDGE COMES FROM THE FUTURE, AND WE CANNOT. AND IT SEEMS TO ME THAT CATARDONE HAS GAINED EIFFEL'S TRUST NOW...

THAT'S WHY WE CAME BACK HERE! IF YOU COULD SUGGEST A FEW SOLUTIONS, PETUNIA AND I WILL BE ABLE TO RETURN AND...

YOU DID WELL TO COME BACK...

BUT YOU WERE WRONG ABOUT ONE THING.

???

YOU DON'T NEED MY ADVICE...

...YOU NEED ME IN THE FUR AND WHISKERS!

GERONIMO, YOU CAN SIT IN THE PASSENGER SEAT...
BUT...

YOU'LL SEE HOW THE SPEEDRAT TAKES OFF WHEN I FLY IT!

CONTACT!

MOLDY MOZZARELLA! I'VE NEVER TRAVELED SO QUICKLY AND WITHOUT THE SLIGHTEST BUMP! BUT WHERE ARE WE?
THIS PLACE LOOKS FAMILIAR TO ME...

WE'RE IN THE TOWER WAREHOUSE. IT'S THE NEAREST POINT WHERE WE COULD LAND WITHOUT ATTRACTING ATTENTION.

PROFESSOR, YOU'RE A GENIUS!
NOW, NOW, I HAVEN'T DONE ANYTHING SPECIAL...

...THE BEST IS YET TO COME.

THE WORK WENT ON NONSTOP FOR DAYS. THE WORKERS HAD TO FINISH THE TOWER; WE HAD TO FOIL THE PLANS OF THE PIRATE CATS, UNTIL...
MARCH 31, 1889
THE DAY OF THE UNVEILING...

WHAT'S GOING ON?
TAM
TAM
TAM

HEY, WHAT ARE YOU DOING? THE **WORK** IS FINISHED!

NOW IT'S FINISHED!

SO, HOW'D IT GO?
EVERYTHING'S UNDER CONTROL!
BUT ARE YOU SURE, TRAP?

OH, COUSIN, DON'T BE SO PERSNICKETY! EVERYTHING'LL BE FINE!
BUT... WILL...

IT BETTER WORK.
HMM...

WE ARE HERE TODAY AFTER TWO YEARS, TWO MONTHS, AND FIVE DAYS OF WORK, TO ATTEND THE BIRTH OF A NEW BEACON FOR PARIS, ONE THAT WILL PROJECT THE CITY INTO THE FUTURE.

HERE YOU HAVE IT... THE EIFFEL TOWER!

OOOHHHHH....

AND WHAT COULD THAT THING BE?
HMM... AT FIRST IT LOOKED LIKE SOME ASPARAGUS, BUT NOW IT LOOKS LIKE A CUCUMBER...

THE RESPONSE IS CHILLY.
THE PUBLIC IS NEVER SATISFIED...

GIVE BONZO THE SIGNAL. IT'S TIME TO PUT OUR PLAN INTO ACTION.
GOOD.
WAIT! LET ME SHOW YOU HOW...

I HOPE BONZO DOESN'T GET DISTRACTED.

FINALLY!

IT'S TIME FOR A BIT OF MOVEMENT!

BOOOM

BOOOM

BOOOM

WHAT'S HAPPENING? IS THIS A JOKE?
I HAVE NO IDEA...

?!

INCREDIBLE. THEY SUCCEEDED...

HEE HEE HEE...

RESIDENTS OF PARIS, BOW DOWN TO YOUR NEW EMPEROR!

EH? WHAT DOES THAT RAT WANT?
HE SAID SOMETHING ABOUT AN EMPEROR, I DON'T KNOW...

YOU STILL HAVE YOUR MASK ON...
AH!

JUST A MOMENT!

AND HERE'S CATARDONE, EMPEROR OF THE CATS! THAT'S ME!

THIS TIME HE'S ALSO REVEALED HIS IDENTITY!
THEY'RE ALL TOO SHOCKED TO DO ANYTHING!
BUT WHAT'S PROF. VON VOLT WAITING FOR?!

HE WAS IN THE TOWER WHEN THERE WERE THE EXPLOSIONS. I HOPE HE'S OKAY!

THE SHAFT POWERED BY THE STEAM ENGINE THAT THE PROFESSOR HAD PUT INTO THE CENTER OF THE TOWER HAD STARTED UP!

TURNING ON ITS OWN, IT WAS MOVING THE PIECES THAT VOLT HAD ADDED, CAUSING THE PARTS THAT WEREN'T NEEDED TO TOPPLE!

ALL OF SUDDEN, IT STARTED TO

SOME MORE...

...AND THE TOWER APPEARED!
THERE IT IS!

-=UGH=-

SEIZE HIM!
SEIZE HIM!

THIS TIME YOU'VE WON, STILTON, BUT WE'LL SEE YOU AGAIN SOON!

I REMEMBER IT BEING STRAIGHTER!
AFTER ALL THOSE EXPLOSIONS, DID YOU THINK THE TOWER WOULD BE PERFECT?

AND HE'S PROF. VON VOLT, WHO ENABLED US TO FOIL THE PIRATE CATS'S PLANS!
MAGNIFICENT!

YOU'VE SAVED MY CAREER! YOU SAVED US ALL!
WHAT ARE YOU SAYING? I ONLY DID THE BARE MINIMUM!

MONSIEUR EIFFEL...

I DON'T FULLY UNDERSTAND WHAT HAPPENED, BUT IT SEEMS LIKE YOU OPTED TO CREATE THE ORIGINAL PROJECT...
-AHEM- YES. I HOPE THE RESIDENTS OF PARIS WILL GET USED TO THIS "ASPARAGUS."

I'VE HEARD PEOPLE SAYING THAT THE TOWER ISN'T SO BAD...
THAT MAY BE. BUT IT'S IMPORTANT NOT TO GET TOO FOND OF THIS TOWER. IT WILL BE TORN DOWN IN 20 YEARS.

THEY TOOK TWO YEARS TO BUILD IT AND THEY ALREADY WANT TO KNOCK IT DOWN?
THEY CONSIDERED DOING THAT, BUT THEN THE CITY DECIDED TO KEEP THE EIFFEL TOWER AS A SYMBOL OF PARIS.

ARE YOU REALLY SURE ABOUT THAT, MONSIEUR ALPHAND? I WOULDN'T BET MY WHISKERS ON IT!

I'M LEAVING IN A FEW DAYS TO BUILD A BRIDGE. WOULD YOU LIKE TO COME WITH ME?
OH, I APPRECIATE THE OFFER, BUT I'M MORE OF A LABORATORY GUY, OR RATHER A LAB RAT!

IF YOU NEED HELP, I'M HERE!
NO, TODAY'S CRASHES ARE ENOUGH FOR THE REST OF MY CAREER, THANKS!

ALL THAT REMAINED FOR US WAS TO RETURN HOME...
HA HA HA!
HA HA HA!
HA HA HA!

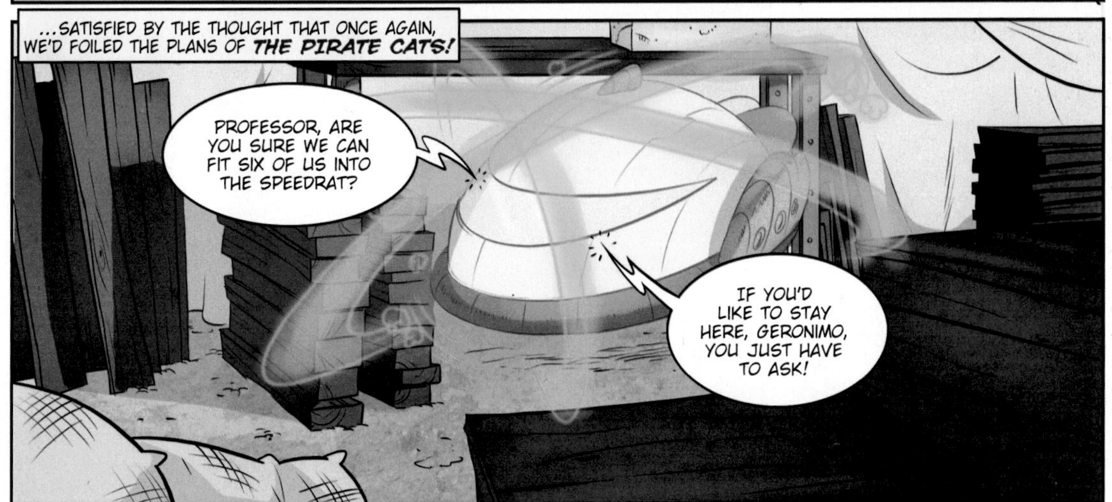
...SATISFIED BY THE THOUGHT THAT ONCE AGAIN, WE'D FOILED THE PLANS OF THE PIRATE CATS!
PROFESSOR, ARE YOU SURE WE CAN FIT SIX OF US INTO THE SPEEDRAT?
IF YOU'D LIKE TO STAY HERE, GERONIMO, YOU JUST HAVE TO ASK!

WE DID IT AGAIN THIS TIME!
PROFESSOR, YOU SHOULD COME TRAVELING WITH US MORE OFTEN!

IT'S BETTER IF I DON'T. SOMEONE NEEDS TO STAY IN THE PRESENT TO MONITOR THE SITUATION. YOU NEVER KNOW!

FINE, THEN WE'LL GO...

UHM... THERE'S JUST ONE PROBLEM, PROFESSOR...

WHAT IS IT, UNCLE?
DO WE REALLY HAVE TO TAKE THIS TRAIN?

GERONIMO! YOU'RE INCORRIGIBLE!
HA HA HA!
MY DEAR RODENT FRIENDS, FAREWELL UNTIL THE NEXT ADVENTURE... ANOTHER WHISKERFUL OF AN ADVENTURE WRITTEN BY STILTON... Geronimo Stilton!

Watch Out For PAPERCUTZ

Welcome to the ebullient, edifying, Eiffel-centric, eleventh GERONIMO STILTON graphic novel from Papercutz—the people dedicated to publishing great graphic novels for all ages. And before I forget, allow me to introduce myself—I'm Salicrup, *Jim Salicrup* the Editor-in-Chief of Papercutz. At this moment, I'm more than a little jealous of a certain time-traveling Editor of The Rodent's Gazette. Let me tell you why…

While I enjoy witnessing Geronimo Stilton's adventures through the pages of our Papercutz graphic novels, Geronimo is the one actually having the adventures! I mean, **MOLDY MOZZARELLA**, man! That mild-mannered mouse has the ability to not only travel anywhere at all in the world, but to any time as well! That's just incredibly awesome when you stop to think about it! So, I do get a bit of wanderlust seeing all the fantastic places Geronimo visits. While I've never been to Paris, France to see the Eiffel Tower, I have been to Eiffel Tower at the Kings Island amusement park in Mason, Ohio—but it's really not fair to compare (there are so many more rides at Kings Island).

I guess the way I deal with my wanderlust is through comics. At the new palatial Papercutz offices, I'm often transported to New Mouse City to Never Land to the world of Ninjago to the Smurfs Village to Whale Island! What, you've never heard of Whale Island? Oopsie! That's because I forgot to tell you our really BIG news:

Coming April 2013, Papercutz will be publishing an all-new THEA STILTON graphic novel series! But the series may not be what you suspect! It stars the Thea Sisters, five fun, lively students at Mouseford College, who want to be journalists like their hero, Thea Stilton (See, that's surprising!)! In the first graphic novel, you'll discover "The Secret of Whale Island"! And just to whet your appetite, we're presenting a special preview on the following pages.

All-new, full-color Graphic Novel
Thea Stilton
THE SECRET OF WHALE ISLAND
PAPERCUTZ

You know, I bet ol' Geronimo may be a little jealous of me! After all, through the magic of Papercutz graphic novels, I get to visit all sorts of incredible places, and I never have to leave my office—and I never have to deal with those pesky Pirate Cats! And the same can be true for you too! Just let Papercutz be your passport to adventure! (Note to self: Send Geronimo a box of Papercutz graphic novels—he deserves some risk-free fun!)

Thanks, Jim

Caricature of Jim by Steve Brodner at the MoCCA Art Fest.

Special preview of THEA STILTON Graphic Novel #1 "The Secret of Whale Island"!

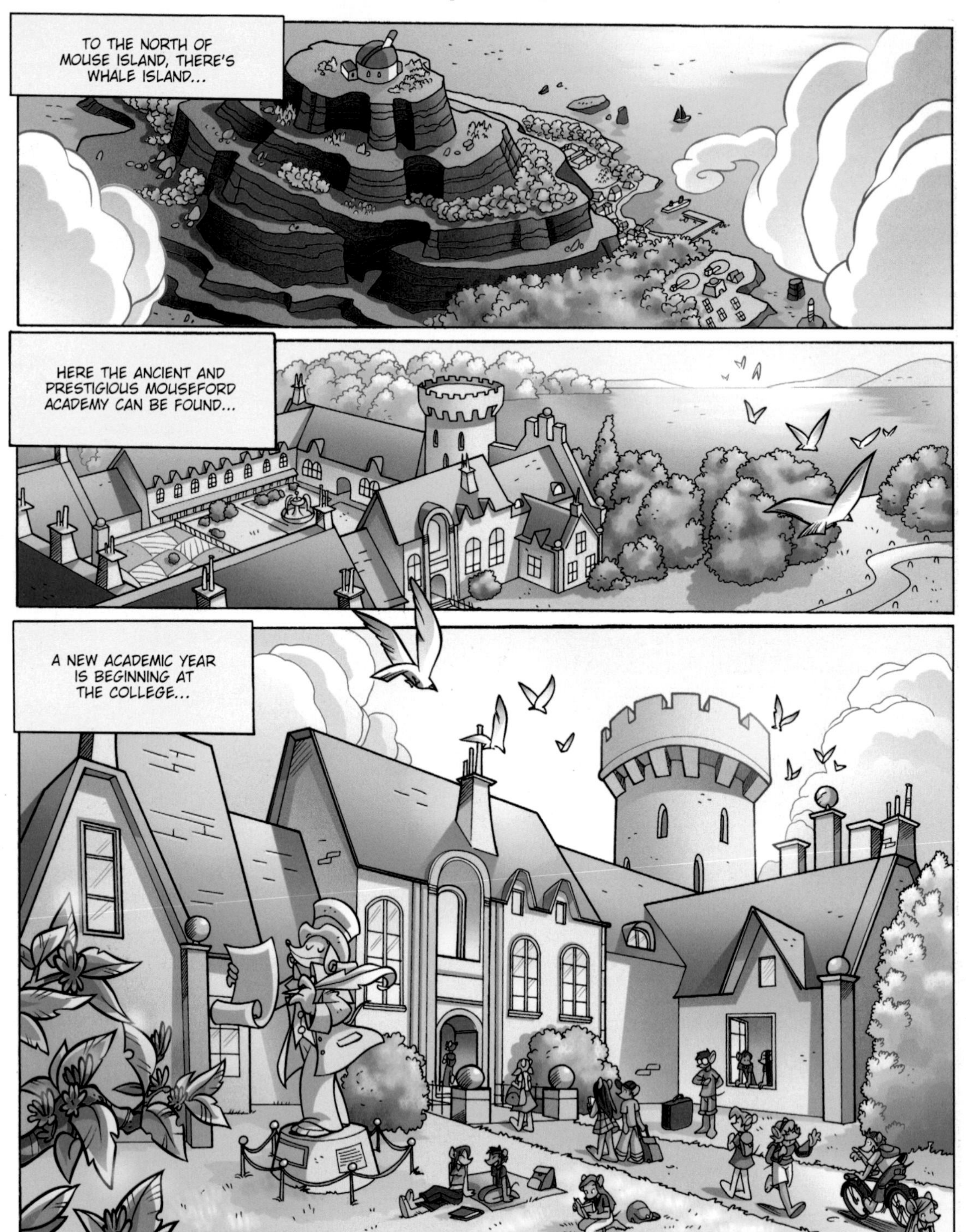

ACCORDING TO TRADITION, THE START OF COLLEGE CLASSES COINCIDES WITH THE ARRIVAL OF THE WHALES IN THE SEAS AROUND THE ISLAND...

MEANWHILE, IN THE STUDY OF OCTAVIUS DE MOUSUS, THE HEADMASTER OF MOUSEFORD ACADEMY...

"DINA HAS DONE IT! SHE'LL BE THE FIRST WHALE ISLAND RESIDENT TO ATTEND MOUSEFORD!

DON'T DO THAT, MOM! THE COLLEGE IS NEARBY...
I'M SO PROUD OF YOU! ~SNIFF SNIFF!~

CONGRATS, BIG SIS!
OH, HOW NICE OF YOU! THEY'RE BEAUTIFUL, MARINA!
YOU KNOW... ONE DAY I WANT TO GO TO COLLEGE LIKE YOU!
YOU'LL DO IT, I'M SURE! ~SMACK!~

THE WHOLE TOWN CAME BY TO CONGRATULATE DINA! EVERYONE CAME TO WISH HER FAREWELL, OVERWHELMING HER WITH COMPLIMENTS AND PRESENTS...
HURRAY FOR DINA! YIPPEE!

THEY'RE ALL HERE... EXCEPT JOHN-LEOPOLD!

COMING THROUGH! EXCUSE ME! MAKE WAY FOR THE DANCE DRESS!
OOOH!
AN ENCHANTING DRESS!
IT'S AMAZING!

WHO'LL BE YOUR DATE?
REALLY, WHO? DINA'D HOPED SHE COULD DANCE WITH JOHN-LEOPOLD... BUT PERHAPS IT WASN'T TO BE!

Don't Miss THEA STILTON Graphic Novel #1 "The Secret of Whale Island"!

THE PIRATE CATS TRAVEL TO THE PAST ON THE CATJET SO THAT THEY CAN CHANGE HISTORY AND BECOME RICH AND FAMOUSE, BUT GERONIMO AND THE STILTON FAMILY ALWAYS MANAGE TO UNMASK THEM!